Mary & Joseph AND THE Baby & Me

Straight from the Donkey's Mouth

Jeff Bates & John Ritter

WestBow Press books may be ordered through booksellers or by contacting:

WestBow Press
A Division of Thomas Nelson & Zondervan
1663 Liberty Drive
Bloomington, IN 47403
www.westbowpress.com
1 (866) 928-1240

ISBN: 978-1-9736-0574-4 (sc)
ISBN: 978-1-9736-0573-7 (e)

Library of Congress Control Number: 2017915281

Print information available on the last page.

WestBow Press rev. date: 5/18/2018

WESTBOW
PRESS®
A DIVISION OF THOMAS NELSON
& ZONDERVAN

Prelude

It's Christmas, it's Christmas-
our favorite time of year,
With Jingle Bells, Santa Claus, and that
famous red-nosed reindeer.
How did Christmas come to be? That's
what this story's all about.
And you're going to get it straight
from the Donkey's mouth.

They needed to leave for Bethlehem, but
Joseph just couldn't decide
Which animal he should choose to give Mary a comfy ride.
"Horses are too tall," he said, "And camels are too lumpy,
But a donkey rides just right when the road gets a little bumpy."

Then I heard him call, "Hey, Donkey, meet me at the gate!
Mary's having a baby soon and we just can't be late.

He loaded me up and he
weighted me down,
'Til my tummy almost
touched the ground.
We were such a sight to see-
Mary and Joseph and
the baby and me.

Mary sat upon my back, while
Joseph held the reins.
The road was rough and rocky,
but none of us complained.
At night, we stopped to build a
fire and have a bite to eat.
We tried our best to get some rest,
but none of us could sleep.

Then Mary felt the baby jump and
said, "He's coming soon."
Joseph said, "The baby's comin'?
We have to find a room!"
"Hurry, Donkey, hurry! Kick it up a notch!"
"Joe, Let's hit the road; I'll give it all I got!"

Step by step and hoof by hoof,
we made it into town.
We knocked on every door, but
each place turned us down.
At last, a nervous innkeeper said,
"I have no room for you,
But if you're okay with a little hay,
maybe my stable will do."

He rushed and fussed like crazy to
make everything just right.
He brought water, towels, and blankets
and fresh hay for the manger that night.
Then Mary smiled and thanked
him for making it so clean.
And I wondered why she said,
"It's a bed fit for a king."
A king ? A king ? How could that possibly be?
With Herod sitting on the throne,
it made no sense to me.

While I was lost in donkey
thoughts, I heard a little cry.
Then suddenly the night lit up with
a bright new star in the sky.
When I turned and saw the baby
my heart was filled with joy.
There was something special
about Mary's little boy.
My eyes filled up with happy tears
when I heard the angels sing.
Suddenly it came to me–
He really was a king.

I knew they needed rest, so I
took a good long walk
And I came upon some shepherds
listening to an angel talk.
He said, "Tonight a Savior is born,
right here in Bethlehem."
Then I learned who Jesus was as
the Angel spoke to them—
God's one and only Son sent
from heaven above
To be our friend, to guide us,
and to fill us with His love.

The shepherds hurried and scurried,
each wanting to be first
To worship Christ the King and
tell of His wonderful birth.
I followed and saw them fall to their
knees as the baby smiled at them.
Then I knew why God had hung the
star to lead others here to Him.

Suddenly I heard a noise and I
stepped outside to see
Three Wise Men bringing gifts,
following the star from the east.
They spoke of King Herod, a
wicked, scheming man,
Who'd even sent a soldier to track
them through the desert sand.

Herod wanted to know where
to find the newborn king;
He'd ordered them to come back
and tell him everything.
But an angel of the Lord came and
warned them in a dream:
They should not trust King Herod,
but avoid his evil scheme.

I showed them to the stable,
then, in the corner of my eye,
I saw the sneaky soldier hiding
behind a tree nearby.
I snuck up on the soldier and,
at just the perfect time,
I gave him a big old donkey
kick right in his behind.
He flew through the stable door
and landed at the manger.
The baby Jesus laughed and
giggled at the silly stranger.

Then suddenly the soldier forgot
why he was even there
As soon as he saw the Savior,
he let go of every care.
He bowed his head to worship,
his heart forever changed.
I knew right then that none of
us would ever be the same
The wise men gave Him their gifts
on that first Christmas day,
Rich gold, frankincense, and myrrh
they placed on the humble hay.

The cattle started lowing and made a happy noise.
What a celebration! I hee-hawed with joy.
The shepherds and their sheep joined in to sing His praises,
The first carols to be sung throughout all the ages.

Now you know the story of how Christmas came to be
With Mary and Joseph and the Baby and me.

9 781973 605744